DC SUPER HERO
FAIRY TALES

BATMAN'S HANSEL AND GRETEL TEST

by Sarah Hines Stephens
Illustrated by Agnes Garbowska
colors by Sil Brys

BATMAN CREATED BY
BOB KANE WITH BILL FINGER

STONE ARCH BOOKS
a capstone imprint

Published by Stone Arch Books, an imprint of Capstone
1710 Roe Crest Drive, North Mankato, Minnesota 56003
capstonepub.com

Library of Congress Cataloging-in-Publication Data
Names: Hines Stephens, Sarah, author. | Garbowska, Agnes, illustrator. |
Brys, Silvana, colorist.
Title: Batman's Hansel and Gretel test / by Sarah Hines Stephens ;
illustrated by Agnes Garbowska ; colors by Sil Brys.
Description: North Mankato, Minnesota : Stone Arch Books, an imprint of
Capstone, 2022. | Series: DC super hero fairy tales | Audience: Ages 8–11. |
Audience: Grades 4–6. | Summary: In this twisted retelling of "Hansel and
Gretel," Robin and Batgirl are out on a training test to find their way back to
the Batcave, but when they stumble upon a cottage made of corn, they must
also use their wits to escape a frightful foe.
Identifiers: LCCN 2021029821 (print) | LCCN 2021029822 (ebook) |
ISBN 9781663959065 (hardcover) | ISBN 9781666328356 (paperback) |
ISBN 9781666328363 (pdf)
Subjects: LCSH: Batgirl (Fictitious character)—Juvenile fiction. | Robin,
the Boy Wonder (Fictitious character)—Juvenile fiction. | Scarecrow
(Fictitious character from DC Comics, Inc.)—Juvenile fiction. | Batman
(Fictitious character)—Juvenile fiction. | Superheroes—Juvenile fiction. |
Supervillains—Juvenile fiction. | Survival—Juvenile fiction. | CYAC:
Fairy tales. | Superheroes—Fiction. | Supervillains—Fiction. | Survival—
Fiction. | LCGFT: Superhero fiction.
Classification: LCC PZ8.H544 Bd 2022 (print) | LCC PZ8.H544 (ebook) |
DDC 813.6 [Fic]—dc23
LC record available at https://lccn.loc.gov/2021029821
LC ebook record available at https://lccn.loc.gov/2021029822

Designed by Hilary Wacholz

Printed and bound in the USA. PO4608

TABLE OF CONTENTS

ONCE UPON A TIME . . .

THE WORLD'S GREATEST
SUPER HEROES COLLIDED WITH
THE WORLD'S BEST-KNOWN
FAIRY TALES TO CREATE . . .

DC SUPER HERO
FAIRY TALES

Now, Batgirl and Robin must find their way back to the Batcave. But the training test turns tricky when they stumble upon a creepy corn cottage and a frightful foe in this twisted retelling of "Hansel and Gretel"!

CHAPTER 1

LOST IN THE WOODS

SCREEEEECH!

The tires of Robin's motorcycle squealed as he tore through the streets of Gotham City.

"You're almost there!" Batgirl told him through the communicator in his ear. "I'm sending the exact coordinates now."

Numbers appeared on the small screen Robin wore on his wrist. With the touch of a button, he sent them to the tiny drone clinging to his backpack. The drone flew off.

From a remote location, Batgirl took over. Using images from the drone's camera and the controls on her computer, she piloted the small device. It carefully picked up a metal object perched on top of Gotham City's tallest building.

"Got it!" Batgirl reported.

Robin touched his wrist screen again. The drone quickly headed for home.

"Yes! Regroup at the Batcave!" Robin said as he twisted the throttle.

The two young Super Heroes made their way as fast as they could to the secret underground lair. Batgirl stepped into the Batcave just as Robin was getting off his motorcycle.

Batgirl checked the time. "Five minutes faster!" she panted out.

Batman stood in the large space with his arms crossed over his chest. "You've done well," he told his two apprentices.

As tirelessly as the Dark Knight fought evil, he also trained Robin and Batgirl to be top-notch crime fighters. Recently, Batman had been hiding objects around Gotham City for them to uncover. They had been getting faster with each trial. This one had hardly been a challenge at all.

"But I think it's time to test your skills in a new way," Batman went on. He looked over at the table where the drone had landed. "I want you to give me all of your tools and technical equipment."

Robin raised an eyebrow, but he removed his wrist screen and the gadgets from his Utility Belt. He handed them to his mentor. Batgirl did the same.

"I don't understand," Batgirl said. She knew that Batman prized all the high-tech devices that his trusted butler, Alfred, created. "Why do we have to give them up?"

"Alfred's tools make fighting crime much easier, but you cannot depend on them. You must be able to get out of any scrape relying on nothing but your wits," Batman explained. "So, I'd like you both to get lost. In fact, I am going to lose you myself."

Robin laughed. "Are you going to take away our tools, blindfold us, and drop us in the middle of nowhere?" he joked.

Batman held up two blindfolds. "That's exactly right, Robin," he said. "I want you and Batgirl to be able to make your way back to the Batcave from *anywhere* without assistance."

"Wait, you're serious?" Robin asked.

Batgirl smiled. Batman was a tough teacher. However, she and Robin were no strangers to hard work. They never hesitated to take on whatever challenges the Dark Knight threw at them. But this was certainly a new twist.

"What about food? Or nontechnical supplies?" Batgirl asked. "Will we have those?"

"All you will have are the clothes on your body. When push comes to shove, our bodies and brains are all we have," Batman told the pair. "So that's all I shall send you out with. I'm certain that's all you will need."

Batgirl and Robin looked at their mentor and then at each other. They wished they felt as confident as he did!

Without further delay, all three Super Heroes boarded the Batcopter. Robin and Batgirl put on their blindfolds. Then Batman lifted off. Half an hour later, the chopper touched down.

"When you can't hear the Batcopter anymore, you may remove the blindfolds," Batman instructed Batgirl and Robin after helping them out. The pair stood shoulder to shoulder.

CHOP·CHOP·CHOP

The Batcopter kicked up dust and wind as it took off. The sound of whirring blades echoed for a long time. When the noise finally faded, everything felt strangely silent.

Batgirl and Robin removed their blindfolds and blinked in the light. They stood in a clearing in a forest.

The two heroes immediately began looking for clues to their whereabouts.

"Well, the sun is setting over there," Batgirl said. She pointed to the sun as it sank below the tall tree line. "So we know that way is west."

Robin inspected the trees. They all had moss on the same side. "It's not a guarantee, but moss often grows on the shadier side of trees. So I would say this way is north," he said, pointing. "But what we don't know is which side of the city we're on."

Robin heard a twig snap and turned to see Batgirl pulling herself up a tree. She was trying to get a better look around.

"Can you see anything?" Robin asked.

"Just more trees!" she shouted. "I'm going to climb higher!"

Batgirl reached for the next branch. The limbs were getting smaller the farther she climbed. The tree began to sway under her weight. Still, she could not make out anything beyond the dense forest. She went even higher.

CREEAAAK

The tree groaned and leaned even farther. Suddenly the branch beneath Batgirl gave way.

CRACK!

The hero plummeted. She started to reach for her grapnel in her Utility Belt, but then she remembered her tools weren't there! She crashed down, snapping two smaller branches before grasping a bough sturdy enough to stop her fall.

"Ouch," Batgirl muttered.

She was scraped and sore but okay. Slowly, she climbed the rest of the way down to stand beside the Boy Wonder.

"What I wouldn't give for a computer!" Batgirl said. "A GPS device would make this a snap."

"I guess we're more dependent on our gadgets than I thought," Robin admitted. "We could start walking in one direction until we come to a landmark."

"We might end up walking in the opposite direction of where we want to go, but it's our best option," Batgirl agreed. She pointed west and raised her eyebrows. "This way?"

Robin nodded and cut a path toward the setting sun. Batgirl walked behind him, making sure they stayed on course by noting the moss and light.

Batgirl also kept her eyes peeled for clues. She listened for running water or traffic or planes flying overhead—anything that might hint at which direction Gotham City lay. All she heard was wind and the tweeting of birds.

"Robin, stop!" she suddenly blurted. "Listen!"

Robin froze. He held completely still as he strained to hear. He looked at Batgirl, confused. "All I hear are birds."

"Yes!" Batgirl said. "Exactly."

CHAPTER 2

CORN MAZE

The two Super Heroes were lost in the middle of an unknown woods, and the only thing they could hear were bird songs. Yet, a smile bloomed on Batgirl's face.

"That's just it," Batgirl told Robin. "That's the clue we're looking for. I hear cardinals, warblers, herons . . . and I'm almost certain that squawking is a pink-footed goose!"

"Um, okay." Robin still looked confused.

"The pink-footed goose is only found in Europe," Batgirl explained. "But I saw a news report about how several recently flew the wrong way while migrating. They ended up here. They're being cared for at Stanton Bird Sanctuary . . . just south of Gotham City!"

"*Ahhh!*" Robin said, finally getting it. "So that means the Batcave is—"

"That way!" the young heroes said together. They headed north.

The team only had to walk for an hour or so. They reached the offices of the bird sanctuary and were able to get a ride into the city. When they appeared in the Batcave, Batman was surprised to see them.

"You solved that problem much more quickly than I thought you would," said Batman.

"Maybe that's because we're so good at using our wits!" Robin said.

"Perhaps," Batman replied thoughtfully. "Or perhaps it was because I didn't make the task hard enough. Or get you lost enough."

"Oh, we were *definitely* lost," Batgirl said. She jabbed Robin in the ribs when Batman wasn't looking. Her partner's boasting was going to get them sent out again!

But Batman wasn't paying attention. He was focused on his computer. He checked several maps. He brought up weather reports.

"Tomorrow we shall try again," Batman finally announced. "Now, get some rest. I think you're going to need it."

Robin and Batgirl exchanged a look. They knew what this meant. Their mentor was really going to put them to the test!

The new day dawned gray and chilly. The sky was overcast. The sun was nowhere to be seen. After again handing over all their tools, Robin and Batgirl took their blindfolds from Batman. Once more, they boarded the Batcopter and took off.

Yesterday's challenge had been hard, and Batgirl knew that today was going to be even harder! Her ears had provided the clue they needed the day before, so she listened carefully from the moment they lifted up into the air. But the blades spinning loudly overhead drowned out any other sounds.

Robin tried to track their direction by noting which way the craft turned. But Batman kept banking hard to the left and to the right. Robin felt dizzy with the effort.

When the Batcopter finally paused midair, neither of the young heroes had any idea where they might be.

"I can't land here!" Batman shouted to the pair over the engine. "You will need to rappel down!"

"Blindfolded?" Batgirl asked as Batman put a belt around her and clipped it to the line that she would be lowered on.

"You can remove your blindfolds when I'm gone," Batman said.

Both Robin and Batgirl had dropped from helicopters on a line before. It had been part of their training. But neither had attempted it without the use of their eyes!

Robin went first.

ZZZIIIP!

"He's down!" Batman shouted to Batgirl when the rope was released. "You're next."

Batgirl felt for the edge of the craft's open door. She held tight to the rope and the attached braking system. Then she stepped out.

ZZZZZIIIIIIIP!

Batgirl quickly slid down the rope. She started braking almost immediately so she would not land too fast. A moment later, her feet touched solid ground.

With a sigh of relief, Batgirl unclipped the belt and line. Overhead, the sound of thundering blades began to fade.

CHOP CHOP chop chop . . .

Both Robin and Batgirl removed their blindfolds as soon as the sound had faded away to nothing.

Once again, the pair saw they were surrounded by plants. But they weren't in the woods this time. They had been dropped in the middle of a cornfield!

Corn. Corn. Corn. Whichever direction they looked in, all Batgirl and Robin could see was corn.

"Did Batman leave us in a corn maze?" Robin joked.

"A corn maze without a path!" Batgirl said. "If this is a crop, there should be a farm close by. But how are we going to get a look around?"

The tall cornstalks grew over the heroes' heads. Though the plants were sturdy, they could not hold the weight of a person.

"You can climb on my shoulders," Robin said. "That should get you high enough."

Batgirl clambered up onto her partner. Seated on Robin's shoulders, her head rose above the cornstalks. She peered around.

"It's just corn and more corn," Batgirl reported.

"Try standing up," Robin suggested.

Batgirl stood slowly, with her feet on Robin's shoulders. Even so, she could not make out any trees or buildings or landmarks. The only thing Batgirl noticed was that the corn seemed to be releasing a lot of pollen into the air. A hazy cloud hovered over the endless field.

"It's still just corn in all directions," she said. "And a *lot* of pollen."

"I guess we'll have to pick a direction and start walking again," Robin said. He held up his hands to help Batgirl climb down.

AH-CHOO!

Batgirl sneezed suddenly and her foot slid off Robin's shoulder. Luckily the boy caught her with his outstretched arms.

"Whoa. Sorry," Batgirl apologized when she was back on her own two feet. It wasn't like her to slip. She shook her head to clear it. "I think the pollen was getting to me. I got a little dizzy."

"Are you okay?" Robin asked. He didn't say anything, but he was starting to feel a bit woozy himself.

Batgirl took a deep breath. "Yes, I'm fine now. Let's go."

Robin picked a direction and the pair set off, walking single file. The going was slow. The corn was tightly packed. The leaves were rough and scratched their skin.

The cloudy gloom made everything eerie. Both Batgirl and Robin found themselves constantly looking over their own shoulders. They could only see a few inches in any direction—and it all looked the same.

Without the sun or moss to guide them, it was impossible to tell where they were going. So about every twenty feet, Batgirl tore an unripe ear of corn from a stalk. She dropped it to mark their path.

They had been walking endlessly when Batgirl stopped suddenly. "Oh no!" she cried.

At their feet was one of the ears of corn she had dropped earlier.

"We're walking in circles!" Robin said. "We're never going to get out of here!"

Batgirl heard frustration in his voice. And something worse—fear!

Batgirl rubbed her eyes. She wondered if she should tell Robin that she was feeling dizzier than ever. Or that she also felt scared.

Batgirl didn't need to say anything. Robin sensed his partner was feeling off too. The creepy feeling was affecting them both.

"Maybe we should change up our plan," Robin said. "We could sit tight till nightfall and use the stars to guide us."

"We can't do that if these clouds don't clear," Batgirl pointed out. She looked up at the gray sky. "We'll be lucky if we get any moonlight!"

Robin sighed and kicked at one of the cornstalks. It let out a puff of pollen.

"I think there's something funny about this corn and all its pollen," Robin said. "I feel . . . weird . . . and scared."

"Me too," Batgirl admitted.

On the last test, she hadn't been worried. This time, she felt alone and frightened and not at all like herself. She wanted to give up.

But she wouldn't. She couldn't!

"We've *got* to get out of here!" Batgirl cried. "Now!"

CHAPTER 3

CORN COTTAGE

The young Super Heroes turned in a slow circle, looking for something to help them decide which way to go. The endless corn was as frightening as it was frustrating.

"What I wouldn't give for my gadgets right now!" Robin said angrily. "Or anything besides this corn!"

He picked up the ear of corn that marked their path. He hurled it as high and as hard as he could.

Batgirl followed the cob with her eyes as it spun away. Then something else caught her attention.

"Robin, look!" she shouted.

A thin plume of green smoke was snaking its way up and out of the tall plants.

"That smoke is coming from a fixed spot," Batgirl said excitedly. "Which means it could keep us moving in *one* direction."

"True," Robin agreed. "And where there's smoke, there's fire . . ."

"And maybe people," Batgirl finished.

The pair started walking toward the strange green smoke. It seemed like their only choice.

Batgirl rubbed her eyes again as she walked behind Robin through the thick corn. She felt coated in the plants' strange pollen. She was also fighting a growing feeling of doom as they neared the green smoke trail. Her heart pounded. Her head swirled. In front of her, Robin seemed to slow.

CAW! CAW!

A crow whirled overhead, screeching at the pair as they stumbled into a clearing. They staggered to a stop and stared at the sight before them.

The sea of endless corn had opened up at last. There in the small space sat a little cottage made entirely of corn!

Robin walked up to the tiny house. Its walls were made of cornstalks, tightly tied together to make columns as strong as logs.

Batgirl came up beside him. "Is it *all* corn?" she asked.

"I think so," Robin replied. Though the house looked cheerful, like something out of a fairy tale, it was still strangely ominous. "But who would live here? What is it for?"

Batgirl and Robin walked around the small structure, taking it all in. The roof was covered in dried corncobs. A corncob chimney was perched on top, belching out the green smoke. Stacked cornstalks framed windows that were fitted with what had to be corn sugar glass. More dried stalks lined the door, which even had a corncob knocker.

Batgirl and Robin stood frozen in front of the entrance. Neither of them wanted to knock and see who, or what, was inside.

"It's just a house. So why do I feel so frightened?" Robin whispered.

As if in answer to his question, the door of the cottage slowly began to open.

CREEEAAK!

When a gangly figure appeared in the doorway, Batgirl knew exactly where their feelings of fear were coming from.

"Scarecrow!" Batgirl shouted.

The scraggly Super-Villain leered at them and stepped out of the cottage.

"I thought I heard something out here!" Scarecrow cackled. "I wasn't expecting company. But it must be your unlucky day. You've arrived in time to help me with my final steps! I've just finished cooking up my last ingredient."

The sight of the villain sent a shiver up Batgirl's spine. She was familiar with this evil scientist. Scarecrow had faced off with Batman many times and was best known for inducing fear in his victims. He delighted in scaring people . . . to death!

Batgirl crouched, ready for anything. "What exactly are you up to, Scarecrow?" she demanded.

Beside her, Robin was also prepared to spring. "Let me guess," he hissed. "This crazy cornfield is something you created to scare people away from your secret lab? And the pollen is what's been making us feel so strange!"

Scarecrow lunged forward at the pair. Robin flinched and stumbled back. It was not like him to shrink away from danger, but he couldn't help it!

"You seem twitchy." Scarecrow chuckled. "My dread pollen must be working!"

Batgirl shivered again. It was working all right! She looked around anxiously, searching for a way out. There was nowhere to run. If they went back into the cornfield, they would be lost and at the mercy of the pollen's effects.

Did Batman realize he was sending us to Scarecrow's lab? she wondered. *Is this part of the test?*

Either way, Batgirl planted her feet and stood ready to face her foe. Fear or no fear.

Beside her, Robin also took a fighter's stance. He gathered as much courage as he could, then made a move. He dove for Scarecrow's legs. The villain leaped away just in time, and Robin skidded to a stop.

With Batgirl ready to attack on one side and Robin on the other, Scarecrow turned and ran. He went right back into his corn lab, leaving the door open.

Outside, Batgirl and Robin looked at each other. Should they follow? Should they flee?

The fear created by Scarecrow's pollen could not cloud the young Super Heroes' better instincts. They had to stop whatever evil the professor of fear was planning!

The pair charged the door. They burst into a dim lab, but they were stopped in their tracks.

FFFOOOOOOSH!

Scarecrow was waiting and blasted them with a cloud of purple gas. Then everything went dark.

CHAPTER 4

LAB BATS

Batgirl woke up on a corn husk floor feeling groggy. She struggled to sit up. Her hands and ankles were tightly bound. She wiggled on the floor, turning to see the rest of the room.

She was in Scarecrow's laboratory. That much was obvious. She could see a long table on the far side of the room covered in beakers, burners, and bottles of strange substances.

What she could not see was Scarecrow . . . or more alarming, her partner, Robin!

Despite the situation, Batgirl was not feeling hopeless. She was feeling bolder than she had felt wandering through the cornfield. *The pollen must have worn off!* she realized.

Suddenly, from somewhere below the floor, she heard muffled thumps. Then a voice.

"Don't move, Boy Wonder!" Scarecrow shouted down a set of stairs as he backed into the main room. "As if you could!"

Scarecrow has Robin tied up in the cellar! Batgirl thought. She closed her eyes so the villain wouldn't know she was awake just yet. She wanted time to figure out exactly what he was up to.

"Such a perfect test subject for my experiment," Scarecrow muttered to himself. "If I can reduce Robin to a puddle of paranoia with my new terror toxin, I can bring the world to its knees!"

Batgirl listened to the crook's every word as he shuffled around the lab. It seemed as if he had forgotten she was there. Then she felt a cool shadow looming over her.

"And you, clever girl, are going to help me do it!"

"I won't!" Batgirl's eyes flew open and she glared up at the scoundrel.

"Oh, you will," Scarecrow said. He pulled Batgirl to her feet and toward the cellar door. "You see, I need another set of hands to help make my terror toxin. For this mystery mix, timing is everything!"

Batgirl shrank away from Scarecrow's wide, toothy smile. His rotten grimace was horrifying.

"After we have measured and mixed and gotten everything just right, do you know what comes next?" Scarecrow asked. "We try it out on your little friend!"

"You can't make me help you," Batgirl spat back.

"Can't I?" Scarecrow replied. He unlocked and flung open the door to the corn cottage dungeon.

Batgirl's eyes adjusted to the dim light. She spotted Robin tied up in a dark corner.

"See that?" Scarecrow asked.

He pointed to the wall beside the door. Hanging there was a huge gas-blasting tool.

"That fumigator is why you are going to help me. I can use it to fill the whole cellar with a lethal toxin in seconds." Scarecrow cackled. "If you disobey, Bird Brain gets it!"

From his spot in the corner, Robin locked eyes with Batgirl. He tried to tell her without speaking that he was okay. *Do whatever you have to do to get out and get help,* he thought.

Batgirl returned Robin's gaze, but she could not hear her partner's thoughts. Her mind raced. She needed to buy time to figure a way out of this—for both of them!

"Now, come! We have work to do!" Scarecrow said.

WHAM!

Scarecrow slammed the door, locking Robin in the cellar. Then he pulled Batgirl to the table of lab equipment.

Scarecrow untied the hero's hands and chained her to the table. The chains were long enough to allow her to move and do the weird scientist's bidding. But they were tight enough to keep her from escaping.

"This new nightmare mix is going to be my most terrifying brew ever!" Scarecrow bragged. "When the balance is perfect, the ingredients will turn into a gas that I can move easily and release anywhere! No one will be able to escape my nightmare!"

The Super-Villain tapped his bony fingers together, lost in the poisonous possibilities. Then he began to explain.

"This is where you come in, Batty. The ingredients for my masterpiece are unstable," he said. "Not only must they be measured precisely, but three have to be added all at once. It requires more hands than I have."

Batgirl scowled. The last thing she wanted to do was help this crook with his horrible potion. But perhaps there was a way she could sabotage his plan.

She pretended to follow the villain's directions. She measured the required sixteen drops of blue liquid into a test tube. Then, when Scarecrow turned away for a split second, Batgirl added several more.

When Scarecrow turned back, he told Batgirl the next steps. She would pour the blue liquid into a large flask. At the same time, he would add a foul-smelling green powder he had made in the fireplace and another test tube full of a clear *something*.

"Three, two, one!" Scarecrow counted.

They added all three ingredients and . . .

BLOOP!

Instead of turning to gas, the mix turned to muck!

"*AAARRRGGH!*" Scarecrow yelled.

He hurled the flask of useless goo across the room. The glass smashed, making a puddle of ooze and broken bits.

"This isn't right at all!" he shouted at Batgirl. "I thought you were supposed to be smart!"

Smart enough to trick you, Batgirl thought.

"Do it again, and this time count the drops out loud. You must have measured wrong," Scarecrow croaked.

Batgirl counted out the sixteen drops. But once again, Scarecrow looked away to prepare his last ingredient, and Batgirl seized her chance. This time, she poured several drops of the blue liquid onto the floor.

When she added what was left to Scarecrow's other elements . . .

SPLOOSH!

The mix simply sloshed lazily in the glass flask. It was definitely not a gas.

"Curses!" Scarecrow shouted. He tore angrily at his hair. "You're doing this wrong on purpose, aren't you? What do I have to do? Watch you like a hawk?" The patched-together scoundrel suddenly stood up straight. "Or perhaps . . ."

Scarecrow unfastened Batgirl from her chains and threw her into the prison cellar with Robin.

"Wait here," Scarecrow ordered. "When I return, you won't be able to get anything past my eagle eyes."

Batgirl stumbled in the dark, almost slipping on the ground littered with loose corn husks. She rushed to Robin's side.

"Are you okay?" Batgirl asked. She had no idea how long they would have to talk, but she hoped it would be long enough to make a plan.

"I'm fine," Robin said. "Just untie me, quick! I think I have an idea."

CHAPTER 5

LOST AND FOUND

Scarecrow was not gone long. A shaft of
light pierced the darkness as he pulled open
the cellar door. His prisoners, Batgirl and
Robin, blinked up at the light.

"You!" he called, pointing at Batgirl.
"Get up here!"

Batgirl climbed the steps slowly, leaving
Robin in the corner. Scarecrow glowered and
caught her by the wrist when she reached
the top.

"Don't worry, Robin," the villain yelled into the dark. "Batgirl doesn't get to have all the fun. I'll have something special for you next time!"

"I am not your lab rat!" Robin shouted back.

Scarecrow simply laughed and slammed the door.

WHAM!

As Scarecrow chained Batgirl to the table once more, she spotted what he had retrieved from the cornfield. A shabby looking crow was hopping around the work surface. It flexed its greasy wings.

"This is my pet, Croward. He'll be my extra eyes," Scarecrow said. He bent down until he was nose to nose with Batgirl. "So don't try anything . . . or else."

With two sets of eyes now focused on her every move, there was not a thing Batgirl could do to mess up Scarecrow's nightmare mix. But, if everything went according to the plan she and Robin had made, it would not matter. She worked slowly and hoped that down in the cellar, Robin was able to work much faster.

Soon, Batgirl added the precise amount of blue liquid at the same moment that Scarecrow added his green powder and clear substance. This time, the mix did not go gloppy. It did not stay soupy.

FZZZZZZZZ

The brew bubbled for an instant before turning into a nasty green gas. It floated in the bottom of the flask like heavy fog.

"It's perfectly awful!" Scarecrow declared.

He danced around in celebration while Croward flapped his wings. Then the scientist grabbed and held up a tube-like vessel.

"All I have to do is get the gas into this bottle, attach it to the fumigator, and *poof*!" Scarecrow said. "When Robin gets a snoot full of this gas, he'll be scared stiff!"

Batgirl looked over at the cellar door. *Have I bought Robin enough time?* she wondered.

She wasn't sure. So when the villain looked away, she made a grab for the flask.

CAW! CAW! CAW!

Croward sounded the alarm.

Scarecrow whirled. He snatched up the flask of gas. He loaded the toxin into the fumigator bottle while glaring at the hero.

"Give up, Batty. You've lost. But you *have* been a big help," he said in a mocking tone. "You deserve to get an up close look at how this experiment turns out!"

Scarecrow unlocked the cellar door, keeping Batgirl close to his side. Robin stood in the corner with his hands behind his back.

"You don't look very scared . . . yet!" Scarecrow teased the boy.

The crook attached the bottle of gas onto the fumigator.

"Now, watch carefully," Scarecrow told Batgirl. Then his smile grew. "Or better yet, you can experience this for yourself!"

Scarecrow shoved Batgirl. She stumbled down the stairs, coming to a stop near Robin.

"Now I have two lab bats!" the villain crowed.

CLUNK!

He pulled the trigger on the fumigator.

At the same moment, Robin pulled his hands out from behind his back. He was holding two objects. Ever since Batgirl had untied him, the Boy Wonder had been busy—making corn husk masks!

FWWOOOOSH!

A cloud of terror gas began to fill the space. But Robin covered his face with one of the masks. He handed the other to Batgirl, and she quickly put it on too.

They were safe! Earlier, Robin had gathered loose corn husks from the cellar floor to weave together the makeshift gear. The masks could not filter out all of the toxins, however. The pair needed to hurry! They charged up the stairs.

"N-n-no!" Scarecrow sputtered in surprise, dropping the fumigator.

He turned to run, but Batgirl and Robin grabbed the back of his tattered jacket. Then they yanked.

The heroes flattened themselves against the wall as Scarecrow tumbled into the cellar and down into the toxic cloud.

Batgirl and Robin ran up the rest of the stairs. They shut the cellar door and locked it tight.

CAW! CAW! CAW!

Croward flew in frantic circles inside the small lab. He was calling out a warning to no one. The bird's cries were drowned out by screams coming from the cellar.

"I guess Scarecrow's nightmare gas worked," Robin said through his mask.

Batgirl nodded. "And so did our plan! Now there's just one last step."

She went over to the fireplace and built a fresh fire. As soon as a big plume of smoke was rising up into the chimney, the team ran out of the creepy corn cottage.

AAAAAAaaaaaaa!

Scarecrow's shouts grew quieter as Robin and Batgirl pushed through the vast field. They kept the smoke at their backs, so they walked a straight path. And their masks kept them safe from the worst of the dread pollen.

A short time later, the pair burst from the field. They pulled off their corn face coverings. They breathed in the clean air.

Just then, the wind kicked up, and the Batcopter flew into view! Ropes dropped down from the hovering craft.

Robin and Batgirl gratefully pulled themselves inside. Batman sat at the controls.

"You definitely lost us good that time!" Robin told their mentor as they buckled in.

"Did you know what we were going to find in that cornfield?" Batgirl asked.

Batman listened silently as they filled him in on Scarecrow's dastardly deeds. When they had finished, the Dark Knight radioed Police Commissioner Gordon to collect the crook. Then he finally spoke to the pair.

"I admit, I thought the field was strange. But I had no idea that Scarecrow was waiting in the middle of it!" Batman told them. "When you didn't make it back as quickly as last time, I activated the microtrackers I had placed on you in case of emergency. I was coming to check on you."

"But I thought we weren't allowed to use technology to work our way out of this mess!" Batgirl said.

"You weren't. But I never said *I* couldn't!" Batman smiled beneath his cowl. "Besides, you did more than find your way. You captured Scarecrow and saved countless people from his nightmare gas. I would say you've passed my test and then some!"

Batgirl and Robin exchanged a look. Batman was right. Using only their bodies and brains, they had certainly found their way. As the Batcopter whirred toward the Batcave, the young heroes hoped there wouldn't be any more tests for a long, long time.

THE ORIGINAL STORY:
Hansel and Gretel

Once upon a time, a woodsman and his family didn't have enough to eat. His wife came up with a plan to abandon his two children in the woods. But young Hansel and Gretel overheard and prepared. When their father led them into the woods, Hansel dropped white stones he had collected. The children followed the stones home. The next time the father took them out, Hansel dropped bits of bread. But birds ate up the crumbs. The children were lost!

The two wandered the woods till they found a cottage made of gingerbread. The hungry siblings began to eat the sweet walls when suddenly the door opened. A witch stepped out. She was hungry too—for plump children!

The witch locked up Hansel and forced Gretel to cook for him. Each day the witch checked if Hansel had fattened up. But instead of holding out his finger for the nearly blind witch to feel, the boy held out a skinny chicken bone.

Finally, the witch grew impatient. She'd eat the boy, fat or thin! She ordered Gretel to fire up the oven and then see if it was hot. But Gretel pretended not to know how. The witch said, "Silly girl. You climb in like this." As the witch leaned over, Gretel pushed her into the oven and locked the door.

The siblings left for home. With help from a little duck, the two made it back to their father. His mean wife had gone, and now, with jewels the children took from the witch's cottage, the family could live happily ever after.

SUPERPOWERED TWISTS

Hansel and Gretel's father loses them in the woods on purpose because the family doesn't have enough food. Batman gets Batgirl and Robin lost to test them. Both young duos use their wits to find their way back.

Hansel drops stones and bits of bread to mark his path, while Batgirl drops ears of corn to mark hers.

The witch's house of sweets is built to lure children. Scarecrow's cottage of corn in the middle of a frightful field is meant to keep outsiders away!

Hansel tricks the witch by sticking out a bone instead of his finger. Batgirl buys time to make a plan by messing up Scarecrow's experiment.

The fairy tale siblings work together to outsmart the witch before she can eat them and then make it back home to their father. The two Super Heroes work together to defeat Scarecrow before he unleashes his terror toxin and then get back to Batman.

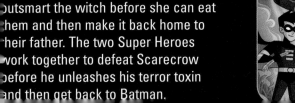

TALK ABOUT IT

1. In your own words, describe how Batgirl and Robin felt about Batman's test. Support your answer with examples from the story.

2. Were you surprised that Scarecrow was in the corn cottage? Why or why not?

3. Batgirl and Robin felt scared as they walked through the cornfield full of dread pollen, but they kept on with their mission. Have you ever felt afraid or unsure but didn't let those feelings stop you from doing something? How did you overcome your fears?

WRITE ABOUT IT

1. Batgirl and Robin didn't have their usual gadgets in this adventure. How did they use just their wits to get out of sticky situations? Make a list of at least three examples.

2. Do you think Batman's test was a good way to train the two young Super Heroes? Write a paragraph explaining your answer.

3. Fairy tales are often told and retold over many generations, and the details can change depending on who tells them. Write your version of "Hansel and Gretel." Change a lot or a little, but make it your own!

THE AUTHOR

Sarah Hines Stephens lives a fairy tale life in Oakland, California, with her two magical kids, a pair of charming dogs, and a prince of a husband. If she could pick a superpower, it would definitely be flight so she could zoom all over the world having adventures, trying out new foods, and visiting far-flung friends and family. Sarah has written more than one hundred books for kids about all kinds of crazy characters—none of whom hold a candle to the wacky cast she loves and lives with.

THE ILLUSTRATORS

Agnes Garbowska is an artist who has worked with many major book publishers, illustrating such brands as DC Super Hero Girls, Teen Titans Go!, My Little Pony, and Care Bears. She was born in Poland and came to Canada at a young age. Being an only child, she escaped into a world of books, cartoons, and comics. She currently lives in the United States and enjoys sharing her office with her two little dogs.

Sil Brys is a colorist and graphic designer. She has worked on many comics and children's books, having had fun coloring stories for Teen Titans Go!, Scooby-Doo, Tom & Jerry, Looney Tunes, DC Super Hero Girls, Care Bears, and more. She lives in a small village in Argentina, where her home is also her office. She loves to create there, surrounded by forests, mountains, and a lot of books.

GLOSSARY

dread (DRED)—causing great fear and anxiety

experiment (ik-SPEER-uh-muhnt)—a test to find out how well something works

fumigator (FYOO-mih-gey-tur)—a tool that releases gas or smoke

mentor (MEN-tur)—someone who teaches and gives advice to a less experienced person

ominous (AH-muh-nuss)—giving the feeling that something bad or evil will happen soon

paranoia (par-uh-NOY-uh)—a feeling that something is out to get you, without any evidence that that's the case

plume (PLOOM)—something that rises into the air in a tall shape, looking somewhat like a large feather

rappel (ruh-PEL)—to lower down from a high spot by sliding down a rope

sabotage (SAB-uh-tahzh)—to damage, destroy, or mess up on purpose

toxin (TOK-sin)—poison

wits (WITZ)—the power to think and decide

READ THEM ALL!

THE AMAZON PRINCESS AND THE PEA

SUPERGIRL AND THE CINDER GAMES

BLACK CANARY AND THE THREE BAD BEARS

LITTLE ROBIN'S FIGHTING HOOD

BATMAN AND THE BEANSTALK

BATMAN'S HANSEL AND GRETEL TEST

AQUAMAN AND THE RAPUNZEL PLOT

SUPERMAN AND THE RUMPELSTILTSKIN RUSE